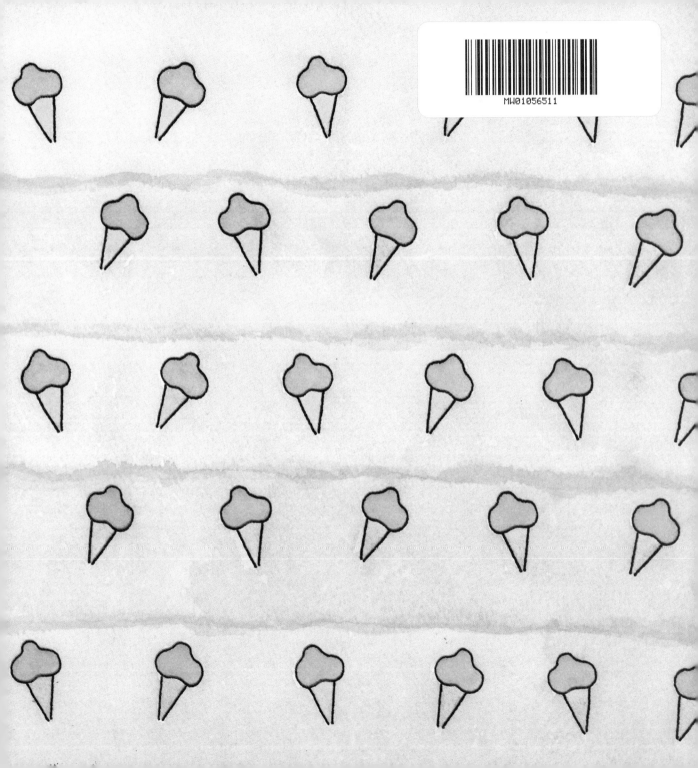

For Ruth and Herb,
who always took us for ice cream
—BRM

For Grace Clarke
—SL

SIMON AND SCHUSTER BOOKS FOR YOUNG READERS
Simon & Schuster Building, Rockefeller Center, 1230 Avenue of the Americas, New York, New York 10020.
Text copyright © 1990 by Brian Mangas. Illustrations copyright © 1990 by Sidney Levitt.
SIMON AND SCHUSTER BOOKS FOR YOUNG READERS
is a trademark of Simon & Schuster Inc.
Manufactured in the United States of America

10 9 8 7 6 5 4 3 2 1

Library of Congress Cataloging-in-Publication Data
Mangas, Brian.   Carrot delight.

SUMMARY: Honey Bunny promises not to bother Father
Rabbit for treats if he will take her on his errand, but
Father Rabbit suffers the denial most.
[1. Rabbits—Fiction] I. Levitt, Sidney, ill. II. Title.
PZ7.M312644Car   1990   [E]   89-11354
ISBN 0-671-67886-8

CARROT DELIGHT

by BRIAN MANGAS
illustrated by Sidney Levitt

Simon and Schuster Books for Young Readers • Published by Simon & Schuster Inc., New York

Father Rabbit tiptoed to the front door. He looked
around before he opened it.
"The coast is clear," he said to himself.
   He turned the doorknob quietly.

"Where are you going, Daddy?" Honey Bunny asked.

"Just to the hardware store," he said. "I'll only be a minute."

"May I come?" Honey asked.

"All right, Honey, but we're not stopping for *anything*," Father Rabbit said. "I have a lot to do today. Do you still want to come?"

"Yes," she said.

"There'll be no ice cream," Father Rabbit said.
"All right, Daddy," Honey said.

"And no park," Father Rabbit added.
"That's okay," Honey said.

Honey Bunny bounced around the house
excitedly.
Father Rabbit went to get his car keys.

Mother Rabbit spoke to Honey Bunny. "Father is very busy today, Honey. Please don't make a fuss about not stopping at the park or for ice cream," Mother Rabbit said.

"I won't," Honey Bunny said.

"Promise?" Mother asked.

"I promise," Honey said.

Father Rabbit and Honey Bunny drove to town.
They counted trucks on the way. Then they counted
station wagons.

"Let's count police cars," Honey suggested.
"There's one now."

Father Rabbit looked in the rearview mirror and
slowed down.

Soon they were in town.
They walked past the ice-cream parlor.

Honey Bunny remembered her promise. She didn't even look inside.

But Father Rabbit looked in and read the sign.

Honey Bunny behaved so well in the hardware
store that Father Rabbit decided to stop for ice
cream after all. When they left the store, Father
Rabbit said to Honey, "How about an ice-cream
cone?"

"No, thank you," Honey answered.

"*What?*" Father Rabbit said.

"I don't want any ice cream," Honey Bunny said.

"But they have Carrot Delight today," Father Rabbit said.

"No, thank you," Honey replied.

"*Why not?*" Father Rabbit cried.

"I don't want any, thank you," Honey said.

Father Rabbit and Honey Bunny got back in
the car. They didn't count trucks or station
wagons on the way home. Then they got stuck
in traffic.

"What's wrong?" Honey Bunny asked.

Father Rabbit got out of the car to see what was the matter. "It's a circus," Father Rabbit said. "Oh, boy!" he cried. "Look at the elephants and the clowns."

Father Rabbit parked the car.
Honey didn't move.
"Aren't you coming?" Father Rabbit asked.

"No, thank you, let's go home," Honey replied.
Father Rabbit got back in the car and they drove
home in silence.

Mother Rabbit greeted them at the front door.
Father Rabbit went inside and moped.
"Did you keep your promise?" Mother Rabbit
asked Honey Bunny.
"Yes, Mother," Honey said.

"You didn't ask to stop for ice cream?" Mother asked.

"No, I didn't," Honey replied.

"You didn't ask to stop at the park?" Mother asked.

"No, I didn't," Honey said.

"That's a good girl," Mother Rabbit said. "Let's go out for a while."

Father Rabbit saw them getting ready to leave.

"Where are you going?" he asked.
"We're going for ice cream," Mother Rabbit said.
"And then to the circus," she added. "Now you can
have some peace and quiet."

"I don't want peace and quiet," Father Rabbit said.

"What do you want?" Mother Rabbit asked.

"I want to have a Carrot Delight ice-cream cone and go to the circus," Father Rabbit said.

"Why didn't you stop when you were out?"
Mother asked.

"It's a long story," Father Rabbit said. "I'll tell you on the way."

The End